LEON COUNTY PUBLIC LIBRARY

3 1260 00623 0281

P9-CCF-342

Elmer Blunt's Open House

by Matt Novak

ORCHARD BOOKS • NEW YORK

Copyright © 1992 by Matt Novak

All rights reserved. No part of this book may be
reproduced or transmitted in any form or by any means,
electronic or mechanical, including photocopying,
recording, or by any information storage or retrieval
system, without permission in writing from the Publisher.

ORCHARD BOOKS
95 Madison Avenue
New York, NY 10016

Manufactured in the United States of America
Printed by Barton Press, Inc.
Bound by Horowitz/Rae
Book design by Alice Lee Groton
The text of this book is set in 21.5 pt. ITC Korinna.
The illustrations are watercolor and colored pencil,
reproduced in full color.

10 9 8 7 6 5 4 3 2 1

Library of Congress Cataloging-in-Publication Data

Novak, Matt.
    Elmer Blunt's open house / by Matt Novak.
        p.   cm.
    Summary: Several animals and a robber explore
Elmer Blunt's home when he forgets to close the door
on his way to work.
        ISBN 0-531-05998-7.—ISBN 0-531-08598-8 (lib. bdg.)
    [1. Dwellings—Fiction.   2. Animals—Fiction.
3. Robbers and outlaws—Fiction.]   I. Title.
PZ7.N867E1   1992   [E]—dc20   91-38424

00623 0281   12-4-92

ak, Matt.

mer Blunt's open house

LEON COUNTY PUBLIC LIBRARY
TALLAHASSEE, FLORIDA

To Victoria

One morning Elmer Blunt overslept.

He was late for work

and did not close the door properly.

Some animals saw the open door

and went into the house.

They explored the kitchen,

the living room,

the bathroom,

and the bedroom.

They heard a noise downstairs

and hid in the closet.

Someone else had discovered the open door.

The thief explored Elmer Blunt's house.

"Furs!" he exclaimed.

"They're ALIVE!" he howled.

He ran down the stairs,

through the house,

and out the door,

slamming it behind him.

That night when Elmer Blunt came home from work,

he said, "I really made a mess this morning!"

So he cleaned every room,

and he went to sleep

in his safe, quiet home.